Fear of Dragon's Fire

Dragon Shifters Motorcycle Club Series Book 1

Ella Hart

Table of Contents

Prologue

You'd think I would be able to forget him. After all, it was so brief. There are plenty of other guys out there.

But, I can't stop thinking about his eyes staring into mine. As if I was precious and beautiful for being what I am.

I can't stop thinking about how his bare skin felt on mine. The blush of the burn from his touch, even when we clasped hands.

The big problem is that I can't stop thinking about either of them.

Blake had been the king of my heart since we were little kids, playing fairy tales in the woods together. He liked to play the beast and tell me to run, and then I'd climb up into a tree and hide from him. I was the better climber, more fearless of heights.

When he saw me way up in the tree, his character changed. He would be Prince Charming, graciously coming to rescue me, and I'd climb down to him. We didn't really know what should happen in the game after that, so we usually went off to try to catch frogs.

Blake was wholesome all-Midwestern honey, with golden-blond hair and deep-brown eyes. He grew up from a mischievous little kid, with a lot of phobias, into a great man with a lot of integrity. I grew up right alongside him, but despite a quick stint as boyfriend and girlfriend in middle school, it took me I went away to college to see him for what he really was.

He was the most beautiful heart I'd ever known. The whole time I was at college I couldn't stop thinking about that noble heart. It's as if he was unbroken and unbreakable. I didn't know how to feel like that.

At least, I didn't know until I met the other one. The one who's very name – very memory – makes my blood heat up until it sears me. Who brings the fire of a blush into my cheeks and whose name still leaves my lips in little moans at night, when I'm not focused on forgetting.

I couldn't forget either of them – which made it impossible to stay.

Chapter One

I came back to town, supposedly there for a summer internship (with Blake's dad, no less, working on aerodynamics in the mountains) after my junior year. Mom showed her happiness at seeing me back from school in her usual way. She hugged me tightly for a super-long time, long enough for my dad to be like, "Okay Stella, you've got to let her go now, so she can go unpack."

Then she held me out at arm's length, and said in a concerned and angry tone, "How is it that a girl can look both as if she's not eating *and* as if she's gained weight?"

I pushed away as gently as I could. "Thanks Mom," I said as my dad winced behind her, "I'll make sure to jot that one down for my therapist."

Mom said, "What? Are we paying for a therapist, now? We're already paying for school."

I tried to move upstairs with my bags as quickly as I could. Blake was waiting for me at the park. We'd decided to be dumb and cute and meet up at the local playground, even though we were both well over the age for that to be reasonable.

It had been almost two years since we'd seen each other. Two years of near-constant, but friendly, texting. Of an unbreakable friendship.

I was exhilarated. I was determined to tear that friendship wide open, by flinging myself at him if I had to.

I had to know. I had to stop being scared of how I felt about him.

Dad was responding to Mom, saying, "I think she means she's going to need a therapist after you called her skinny-fat."

I shouted back from the upstairs landing, not able to resist a retort, "The kids call it slim-thicc nowadays."

Dad shouted back, "I have no idea what that means!" Then his conversation turned into muffled whispering with Mom. I guessed they were arguing about something.

I couldn't care less. I was twenty-two years old, and I'd finally realized that my best friend was the love of my life. After I graduated, we could move into our own little cabin in the mountains and ignore our crazy parents for good. Well, my crazy parents. His mom was just overly-nice, always calling me sweetie and trying to make dinner for us. His dad had got me my internship, so I couldn't complain about him.

I grabbed my purse, ready to run back down the stairs. I was absolutely giddy and, since I'd already caught up with my parents on our way back from Missoula International Airport, I felt I could run out the door without wasting much more time.

The part of me with some sanity and decorum checked the mirror. After all, I'd just gotten off an airplane. That was not a commonly sexy-making travail.

Yes, it was a good call to check the mirror. My hairdo was a lopsided ponytail that had gone from charmingly messy to "Oh no, she needs help." I yanked the hair tie out and tried to fluff up and then smooth down my hair into something reasonable.

That's when my fingers grazed it. A hardened patch of skin on my scalp. I stood very still in front of the mirror, hoping it was just dandruff.

I had no idea what it could be. I'd had dandruff before, but this was, well … scalier. Thicker, as if it was weighty, even though it was only a small patch on the top of my head.

My heart beat faster. In my nervousness about it, it felt as if it was spreading, as I rubbed it. My hair felt thinner in that spot.

I was appalled by it, but not sure what I could possibly do. I snatched my hand away from my head as if it was a burning flame. Whatever it was, it could wait until after my maybe-date with Blake. Plus, as soon as I told my mom I had some weird sort of scalp thing going on, she'd trundle me off to a hospital, no questions asked, to get it x-rayed, inspected, removed, and donated to science. She was efficient like that.

I couldn't wait another second. I rushed down the stairs and faced the parent gauntlet.

They both looked deathly serious as I zoomed past them. I gave them each a quick kiss on the head, but they looked so grave and angry with each other that I stopped my anxious rush.

I said, "What gives? I told you I'd be meeting up with Blake tonight. I'll hang out with you guys all day tomorrow, I swear. It's just the only night that Blake won't be working."

Blake was a nurse in a children's ward, because he's the best person ever and he's amazing with kids. Just thinking about how easily he got along with babies and young kids, even teenagers, made my uterus start applauding.

Dad seemed to make an effort to calm down, but clearly he and mom had been having one of their fights. Mom looked as if she wanted to scream at him.

"We don't have any problem with you going to hang out with Blake," he said, "We just want to talk to you first, Katherine."

I inched toward the door. "Wow, Katherine? My full name? This sounds serious."

Mom snapped, "Let's try to minimize the sass here, Kat. Your father needs to tell you something important."

She was clearly sloughing off the responsibility onto dad. I directed the full force of my whining child voice at him.

"But Dad, I'm going to be late. I know whatever you have to say is really important, and I want to make sure I give it my complete attention and lots of thought. But, I can't really do that right now, with Blake waiting. You always said, a person is as good as their word, and I promised I'd be at the park in like, five minutes."

It worked, as it always did. As soon as Mom ceded the floor to Dad, their battle was lost.

He turned to Mom. "I guess she's right," he said, "It can keep until she gets back, and then we'll have more time to talk about it."

Mom fumed, but she also looked weirdly relieved.

I got out of there as soon as I could. They're weird sometimes, but today was extra weird, and I could not let it wreck my vibe.

I was going to tell my best friend I loved him. Finally.

Just like a fairy tale.

Chapter Two

When Blake walked up, my voice caught in my throat. He looked so masculine and yet so gentle, his broad shoulders and strong chest filling out his soft, blue sweater.

Over the last two years, while we hadn't seen each other, I'd been so worried and imagined that when I finally saw him again, all the magic would have evaporated. But he was, if anything, taller and hotter than I recalled, with even better, softer, fluffier and more golden hair. He'd grown a beard, which I didn't hate, and his eyes were just as enchanting as I remembered.

This was worse. When he walked up, he waved to me with a wide open grin, and I literally croaked like a schoolgirl as I said, "Hi!" back.

I didn't move from my swing. I didn't know how to approach him. In my head he'd already turned into my lover many, many times, but in real life he was some guy I had known since I was a kid.

How do you act in a situation like that? For all my brave self-talk on the plane ride, I was paralyzed by fear.

He stuck a large hand through his belt loop as he leaned back and smiled at me. All of his clothes hung off his meaty frame perfectly. I wanted to ask if he'd turned into a muscled meathead since I'd left, but I didn't want him to know I'd been staring.

"Thanks for coming to hang out," he said in the pleasing, clear voice that I knew had sung choir all through high school. "I know you must be tired from the plane ride."

I had to say something. I tried to tell myself to be playful, like I was when we were still just friends, and as he probably thought I would be now.

Instead, I said snarkily, "Well, try to be interesting enough for me to stay awake."

He looked a little taken aback for a second, as if he was hoping for something else. I sure as hell wished I'd said almost anything but that.

But, bless his heart, he recovered fast, and sat down in the swing next to me. He pretended to ponder, "Hmm. What could I talk about that's more interesting than your and my dad's research? Oh, yes, literally anything."

Now I really thanked God for him. This gave me an excuse to laugh, at least a little, and released some of my tension. I pushed off the ground and called him a jerk, and we started swinging and catching up.

I could barely think, my head was in such an anxious flurry, so all of my responses were trite. It was worse than all the bad first dates I'd ever had. Even a morning after a one-night stand wasn't as bad as this. At least then you could be like, "Get out of my dorm room." I couldn't very well order him out of my life. Not when I wanted him to be more deeply wrapped up in it.

We meandered conversationally through our lives for a bit, sharing small snippets and trying to find jokes or stories, as we usually were able to do over texts. But it was as if everything had dried in person.

I was panicking. I wanted to look at him so badly, it was hard to think.

He was straining for something to talk about, too, I could tell. He kept looking at me and looking at me and waiting for something to happen. I just couldn't figure out the right thing to say.

That's why I was almost glad when a thundering roar kicked up out of the woods around us, blasting down the street. A motorcycle club had burst from the trees and crossed the playground, causing me to scream and tuck my legs up under me on the swing, and Blake to jump up and shout at them.

He called them crazy jerks, but they just hooted and kept going, right onto the road, faster than I'd ever gone in my life. I didn't drive, I pretty much only Uber-ed places, and I couldn't remember the last time I'd actually driven on a highway.

Their breakneck speed was horrifying, but after I had finished screaming, I tried to catch a glimpse of their faces as they zoomed by. One of the riders tried to look at me as well, turning toward me with his helmet blocking his face.

I guess it distracted him, because he lost control of his bike as he hit the edge of the playground. It flipped up and he fell off and rolled on the sidewalk. The bike screeched across the sidewalk.

I thought for sure he was dead. My mouth tasted like blood and my heart beat shot up, like it usually does when I'm scared.

Blake ran right over to him. He leaned down and gingerly flipped up the visor of the biker, probably to see the extent of the damage. After a moment, he jumped up in shock, and then took a couple of steps back. As the biker miraculously rolled over onto his side and stood up, Blake stomped back over to me.

The biker stood on the other side of the playground from the swings, with his helmet under his arm. His leather jacket and black skinny jeans stuck to his lean form. He looked like a dancer, maybe, or an acrobat. Someone with some muscles, but who was more focused on grace than girth.

He had black hair and dark-brown skin, with a smooth, innocent face that held a grin that was anything but innocent. He looked as if he'd just played a fun practical joke on us.

As Blake stormed back over to me, biker guy had the audacity to wink at me, and then he grabbed his bike. He lifted it up with no trouble, even though I could tell it was heavy duty machinery.

As he righted his bike, I caught a glimpse of his jacket insignia, even though he was a long way off. It looked like a snake, maybe? Or a sparkly red dragon.

Blake was standing next to me by the swings, waiting for the guy to go. He blew us a kiss before getting on his bike. I wasn't 100% sure who it was meant for, and then he drove away. He didn't gear up slowly, either. He was off like a cannon, following his disappeared pack down the road.

Blake looked pissed off. I pointed that out, not sure what the guy could have done to make him so angry.

Blake told me, "When I opened his visor, he had his lips puckered up. I thought it was a weird trauma thing, so I ignored it. I checked him for a pulse, and then he whispered that only true love's first kiss could break the spell. He was fine the whole time. What an asshole."

I thought that was hilarious, but judging from Blake's face, I didn't dare laugh. I just looked off down the road and wondered where the motorcycles were headed to.

Chapter Three

We walked back to my house in a stifling and awkward silence. The brief encounter with the biker gang had washed away whatever good mood Blake was in. I wasn't in any place to cheer him up.

My heart was freaking out. It got so the pounding in my chest was drowning out my shouting thoughts. Time was running out! When was I going to ask him out? I felt like such a coward, as every step took me farther and farther away from my perfect chance.

I saw the old creaking, lopsided stop sign that stood at the end of my street. My hands started to itch, and I rubbed at them viciously, just for something to do besides curse the day I was born a coward.

My hands actually felt horrible. The itch felt much worse than any itch I'd ever had before. We were almost back to my place, where he would say goodbye, and then we'd hardly see each other over the summer.

I saw my house. It was now or never. I took a deep breath and looked down.

My hands looked nothing like they usually did. Instead, I had monstrous, gnarled lumps of discolored skin that ended with, not fingernails, but …claws?

What the hell was happening? I screamed.

Blake whipped around toward me, and I had the presence of mind, thank God, to cross my arms to hide my disturbing hands.

I must've looked very petulant, because Blake shook his head. However, instead of telling me to chill out, he said, "I know – those asshole bikers at the park have me all jumpy, too. If I ever see that guy again I'll give him the knock on the head the asphalt didn't."

This was wrong. This was all wrong. I stopped walking.

He stopped and looked at me. "Kat?" he asked, friendly concern lighting up his eyes.

His beautiful blond lashes were almost sparkling under the last light of the setting sun. He looked like a birthday cake, with smooth, creamy skin and sweet icing features.

I was hungry as hell, even though I'd had a huge lunch. It felt as if I hadn't eaten in years. My hands burnt as if I'd dipped them in a lake of fire.

He was a pretty perceptive guy, so I couldn't stand there hiding my hands for long before he honed in on them.

"What's up?" he said with a serious tone, "What's wrong with your hands?"

Then he reached out for them. I could've held them up, and let his strong, gentle touch heal them, as he healed people all day.

I couldn't let him see whatever the hell was happening to me. Not when he looked so perfect.

So, I turned tail and ran into the woods behind my house. He was so shocked I don't think he even thought about coming after me, until I was too deep into the trees for him to follow.

Chapter Four

I ran well into the night. I was starving; my stomach growled louder than my horrible crying. It's hard to run while sobbing but I've never been a quitter.

My hands had been this mottled green color that I couldn't understand, but at some point they'd gone back down to a passably human shape. Now, in the dark they, looked as if they might just be dirty, not deformed. I wondered whether I'd imagined how horrible they looked when I was stressed. I was starting to feel dumb for running out into the woods like a wild animal.

My tears flowed harder, whenever I thought about how I'd just skewered all my chances with the guy I'd been in love with for two years. I was a total mess, full on snot-face, when I heard a murmuring out in the forest.

It sounded like people were way out here in the woods. I moved closer, figuring people would be a better option than getting eaten by wolves.

Flickering firelight in the distance caught my eye, while sounds of revelry took over the usual peaceful tones of the forest at night. It was quite the party.

Hell, it was a full on festival. There was a huge number of people out in the woods, all dancing and scream-talking in the firelight. I wondered what morons lit a fire in the woods during the summer, but given I had just ran into the woods, after imagining scales on my hands, I wasn't in a position to judge.

I came out into the clearing, lurking at the edge of the crowd, and trying not to gasp like a country hick at what I saw.

It was like a college party, but even more stupid and dangerous. People were throwing caution (and their clothes) to the wind. It seemed there was a lot of leather, alcohol, and bad decisions all gyrating on top of each other.

A lot of *leather*? My weary mind put it all together. It was the biker gang I had seen earlier!

I got a look at a jacket and realized I wasn't wrong with my guess. It was a spiraling, serpentine dragon with massive wings, above which I read in medieval-looking letters, "Flamethrowers."

Kind of a simplistic name for a dragon, but I guess the general idea was that these guys and gals caused a lot of destruction.

They were tossing all kinds of shit into the raging flames. A lot of it looked clearly stolen, and everyone's trash was going into the massive bonfires as well. One guy took a full whiskey bottle and threw it in with a smash, which made a huge roar that everyone cheered along with.

People were dancing on top of pickup trucks and SUVS in various stages of undress. I saw one girl sloppily fall off a big SUV and then giggle as she tried to stand up out of the mud.

At least everyone was having a good time. Thankfully, nobody seemed to notice me, because they were all focused on their own enjoyment.

I smelled something wonderful. They were roasting meat on an open flame. From the size and scent of it, it was venison.

I didn't know biker gangs also hunted, but I guess there was a lot I didn't know about this gang, at the time. Such as how literal that "Flamethrowers" name was.

I walked casually toward the food, my stomach roaring and begging for protein.

I was almost pushed over by two guys running by me towards a keg, and I regained my balance by grabbing onto the seat of a motorcycle beside me. I looked at the bike and saw a man and a woman wrapped up.

My face burnt, and I looked away and I hurried away as quickly as I could. I didn't get a great look, but they sure looked as if they were very, very close at the waist.

There was no way, right? That they were going at it on a bike in the middle of this party?

I hurried toward the roasting food, which smelled wonderful enough to kick all images of canoodling bikers out of my head. I was looking around for a fork and plates when a big drop of saliva fell out of my mouth.

I smelled the air and looked down. A slender hand had pushed a skewer of meat underneath my nose.

I reached out to grab it, but I wasn't fast enough. He pulled it away and held it aloft, and I turned, with probably the angriest face I'd ever thrown at a stranger.

I was staring at the biker from earlier – the one who'd been thrown from his bike and who had winked at us. He grinned, clearly tickled to run into me again and to be taunting someone.

Firelight flickered against his playful eyes. They were black, but filled with bright light. It was like the joy of living was radiating out of them.

"Hey," he said, "You're the girl who was with that meat-cake earlier."

I stared at the skewer in his hands. "Sorry to crash the party, but since I was in the neighborhood, I figured I might as well drop by."

He shrugged and said, "The more the merrier. You look hungry." He twirled the skewer gracefully between his index finger and thumb. The meat's juice flickered in the firelight.

I said, "I feel near death, to be honest. Mind handing over the meat before somebody gets hurt?"

He laughed, and held the skewer back a little farther from me. "What'll you do for it?" he asked

I didn't really get the question. "I'll pay you, I guess." I still had my wallet on me, and it was only fair that I give them some cash if I was going to steal their food and intrude on their debauched hospitality.

He shook his head, "No, not like that. I meant what'll you *do*. Like, do."

I still didn't really get it, and then he wiggled his eyebrows at me.

I groaned. "Gross, dude, I don't even know you."

He said, "Yeah, you do. I'm the guy whose life your boyfriend saved earlier. I'd say that makes us, like, dating-in-laws."

I said, "Dating in-laws does sound like something they do here in Montana. But your life wasn't saved. You tried to kiss Blake. Who isn't my boyfriend, by the way."

I felt a twinge of pain in my chest.

I continued, probably only speaking aloud because I was too tired to filter myself, "And he's never going to be."

He said, "Sounds sad". And then he wrapped his mouth around the meat on the skewer, letting his lips close softly together, before pulling off a huge chunk slowly, making a big show of taking it into his mouth and chewing with gusto.

When he swallowed, loudly, he licked his lips slowly, before looking straight at me. Then he bit his lip, blissful, and shut his eyes.

His lips looked wet. Plump. Delicious.

I said, "I swear to God, if you don't give me something to eat, I'm going to go cannibal in the middle of your nice party."

He grinned. "Promise?"

But he wasn't dumb. He handed me the skewer, and got started making me another one.

Chapter Five

It turns out he went by CC, and he was none other than the leader of the gang. As I hung out with him and ate and drank whatever he passed into my hands, people approached him with questions and problems, and sometimes he'd answer cryptically, but a lot of the time he just nodded or shook his head quickly and they'd walk away again.

Even with all the craziness around us, he kept focused on me. We'd drift in and out of conversations, and even when we were listening to someone else talk, he'd shoot me conspiratorial looks and funny glances, as if we were the only two people who really got the joke.

I didn't get why he was being so friendly to me, until we were seated on a tree stump with a group of people listening to this wasted guy sitting on his ass in the dirt. He was talking about the first time he ever saw breasts, in person. While the subject matter wouldn't usually interest me, the punchline was that as soon as the girl whipped them out, all of the smooth preparation he'd done in his head went out the window, and he actually booked it away from the car – his car – which he had to go back the next morning to pick up from in front of her parent's place.

I was very drunk, and this was genuinely hilarious. The image of this big burly biker as a twelve-year-old who was scared of boobs was killing me.

CC was cracking up, as well, and I looked at him. That big grin was killing me, too. It was a movie star grin, a "nothing has ever been wrong over here, we're all having a good time" grin.

He leaned toward me, as if he needed support, because he was laughing so hard, and his hand brushed my thigh, I felt the heat of his nearness. His hand only glanced me, but he kept his shoulder pressed against mine. It was all very friendly.

Someone politely asked me who the hell I was and what had brought me to their party.

I looked at my near empty drink, and was too drunk not to tell the truth. "I had a bad date. Real bad. Unrecoverable, run into the woods and hide, bad."

Everyone kindly made sympathetic noises. Especially CC, who cooed, "Aw, that's really too bad," into my ear while his arm wrapped around my shoulders. He hugged me, and then let his hand linger.

Okay, now I understood. CC was trying to get it, right? Why else would he keep trying to touch me, keep listening to me, and keep introducing me to his friends?

One of the girls in the circle said, "Men are trash. What'd your date do, sweetheart?"

"Or what didn't he do?" somebody joked, and got slapped for their trouble.

I said, "He didn't do anything wrong. It was me. I think I misread something or, like, mis-saw something. It scared me, so I ran."

CC was holding me, and looking at me with a serious expression. I hazarded a glance at him. He kept up the eye contact, as if he was trying to puzzle me out.

For all he was clearly coming on to me, I don't think I'd ever felt so comfortable being held by somebody. Everywhere his arm rested on me was thrilling, but it also felt as if…

As if he genuinely liked me. As if he thought I was interesting.

The thought lit a flame in my midsection that spread across my whole body.

Damn. I don't know what turned me on more. The nearness of his lean, graceful body, or the focus in his eyes that showed he was interested in what I was saying.

That's what I liked about Blake, after all. He was always such a good listener.

As I looked into CC's eyes, and we disconnected from the general conversation and made our own little world, I felt as if he both wanted to eat me and talk to me.

We were snuggling now. I marveled at how smoothly he'd transitioned us from friendly chatter to holding each other so closely. His legs were wrapped up in mine, his hands caressed my torso and my shoulder, and our faces were so close I could feel the warmth of his breath.

When he whispered, "Want to take a walk?" I laughed at how blatant a come on it was.

But in the heat of the moment, all I wanted was to be wanted by this beautiful stranger.

Chapter Six

We were alone in the dark of the forest. He was walking a few steps ahead of me, sometimes turning around to walk backwards while we talked. I didn't know where we were going and I didn't care.

There's this Irish folktale about sprites or pixies or whatever, and they appear in forests as beautiful eyes or voices and mislead travelers off the path. Because their beauty is too hard not to follow.

I definitely felt as if each step was a bad idea, but anytime I felt too doubtful or that my common sense might kick in, CC shot me a look from those sparkling black eyes, and I was hooked. He could lead me anywhere, especially with that megawatt grin.

He asked, "So, do you have a job?"

I said, "So, we're doing small talk now? Nice weather we're having. Do you think the Seahawks are going to go all the way this year?"

His head perked up in cute confusion. "Go all the way with whom?"

I laughed. "With the Super Bowl. Do you think the Seahawks will make sweet, sweet love to the Super Bowl?"

He shrugged. "I don't really care about that. I was asking about you."

I was starting to get sleepy and annoyed. "Why? What do you want to know about me?"

He stopped walking. I didn't notice. I bumped into him, and we would have both toppled over, except he caught us.

We stood in the quiet of the forest, me half-laying, half-standing against his strong chest. He had his arms wrapped around me. Those eyes kept pulling me in, and my own gaze kept flickering down to his lips, which were so close to me now.

He murmured, since even an inch of movement would bring our lips together, "Because I'm trying to figure out if you're the same as me. Because it feels as if you are. I can feel your heat."

I was certainly feeling heat. Every part of me was begging for him. My hands were pressed against his torso, and I could feel his hard abs underneath the soft silk of his black t-shirt.

I slid my hands underneath his shirt, and the gasp of air that escaped his lips was as warm as a furnace. I felt his smooth skin and hard muscle, and I rubbed him, dragging my fingernails across his skin.

He looked up and moaned as I dragged nails across his back and then dove my hands into the tight back pockets of his leather pants.

I wanted to forget everything but the heat of his breath and the firmness of his body. Of course, I couldn't forget everything. He pulled his gentle hands through my hair, and I thought I felt them scrape across the part of my scalp that had been messed up earlier.

I jumped back and screamed. He stepped back from me into a defensive pose, with his hands up. He seemed to be waiting for something, as I caught my breath.

Whatever it was that he was waiting for didn't happen, so he relaxed his posture and looked at me quizzically.

He said, "For the record, I tried to gently brush my hand through your hair. You went straight for my ass."

He fell backwards without looking behind him and gracefully caught a tree branch. He pulled himself up onto it and grabbed another one directly above it. He crouched, up in the tree and waited for my response.

I said, "Wow. When I wear leather pants I can barely even walk."

My hands were itching again. My scalp and shoulders, too. The burning feeling was inescapable.

I tried to ignore it. I stood below him, looking up into the tree, and said, "I used to do that when I was a kid. Climb trees. I loved it."

He reclined against the trunk of the tree, perched on one of the larger branches, while he asked, "So why'd you stop?"

That felt like a weird question. "Same reason I stopped eating Lucky Charms. It's kid's stuff."

I felt embarrassed, calling his agile acrobatics 'kid's stuff', but he only smiled.

And then, in a flash, he was gone. He'd pulled himself up higher into the tree and I lost track of him. I stood in the dark of the night for about a minute, trying to enjoy the stillness and not seem desperate.

I heard the high-pitched howling of a wolf from not too far away, and suddenly 'desperate' appeared to be in my best interest.

"Shit," I shouted, "What do I do?"

Wolves generally don't want anything to do with you, but it had sounded like a hunting call, and this far out into the woods they might take you as an easy midnight snack rather than pass you up.

CC shouted back, "Climb!"

The chaotic howling of the wolves propelled me up, as my limbs easily recalled so many years of practice. In less than a minute I was on the same branch as CC. Where I discovered he was making the wolf noises himself. I caught him right in the middle of a good long howl. He grinned at me sheepishly.

I unloaded a string of curse words at him as my adrenaline diminished and turned into anger. I lunged at him, precarious as we were, and swatted at him semi-playfully. I was also genuinely pissed off.

I was already off center, so it was easy for him to grab my violently waving arms and pull me over so I was on top of him. We kissed, against the weighty trunk of the tree. Having to keep our balance was causing us to constantly shift our body weights and to rub against each other more closely and vigorously. At least, the balance thing was a big contributor.

We kissed and pushed our bodies against each other, until we had the same center of gravity. He kissed my lips, my cheeks, and then down my neck as I tightly gripped the ancient bark of the tree trunk. Then he stopped at my shoulder. He pulled my t-shirt up over my head, barely breathing. He didn't continue kissing me all over, but instead just stared at my shoulder.

Then he looked me in the eye, grinning as if he'd just won a raffle.

"You're one of us," he said, "I knew it."

I didn't get what he meant. I was more distracted by how firmly my fingers were able to grip the wood of the tree.

I pulled my hands back to find they had once again changed into monstrous green claws. They'd been sunk into the tree by the lengthy talons that sprung from my fingers.

I looked at them. He saw them too, but kept smiling, which made the whole thing feel worse. I tried to move away from him – from my own body – more of which had turned green and monstrous. In trying to run away, I fell from our branch.

I hurtled toward the ground, screaming, but I'm not sure if I was screaming at the fall or at my own disloyal limbs.

Chapter Seven

In midair the strangest thing happened. I assumed that I was in shock, or I'd already passed out and started dreaming, or I was dead.

But my fall slowed. My back felt as if I'd been branded on both shoulders, but from out of that vicious burn, suddenly there was a cooling blast of wind.

I not only slowed, but started moving sideways … Instead of falling straight down, I found I was gliding through the forest. Once I realized it was happening, I started to fall again.

Only to feel strong arms wrap around my chest. And then I was off again, gliding through the trees, gracefully avoiding branches and coming up in the air. We broke through the top of the tree line.

I say 'we' because I'd looked up to see the face of whatever had grabbed me. It had a long face, like a horse, except that I'd never seen a horse with razor sharp teeth like it had. And I'd never felt steam coming from a horse's nostrils.

I opened my mouth to say something not very poetic, such as "What the hell is happening right now," but when I opened my mouth, I saw my own nose (or snout). It was as if someone had slapped a mask on me.

My face was clearly as long – if not longer – than the face of the thing that was carrying me. My tongue felt about a foot longer than I was used to.

I had no idea how to speak with it. When I tried, all that happened was some high-pitched squealing. That seemed to amuse the horrific face of the massive creature carrying me.

A voice in my head said smoothly, "Horrific is a little rough, considering you look exactly like me."

Back to high-pitched squealing. The thing holding me rolled its eyes.

I thought, as clearly as I could, "What the actual fuck? Are you reading my thoughts?"

He nodded. How did I know it was a 'he'? The eyes.

Those beautiful, black-as-coal, yet vibrant-as-a-star eyes.

Whatever I was looking at, CC was in there.

The strange voice in my head said, "Telepathy. It's a dragon thing. Nobody's really figured out how to speak with mouths like these, and there's not much point, when we can do the whole telepathy thing."

I was glad we couldn't talk with these mouths. Because I'm pretty sure I would've sounded moronic as I stuttered out, "D-d-d-d-d-dragon?"

CC was soaring, both physically and metaphorically. He was elated, and the voice in my head made me feel what he was feeling in this intense, empathy-plus-one-hundred-way.

In my head he said, "I knew you were like us. As soon as I saw your hands. Well, your hands, but also the way you looked at the shish kebab. I could tell you were my kind of monster, but I wasn't sure. Now it's official."

I tried to say, "I'm not a monster," but my mind only said, "I'm a monster."

He looked bored. He said, "Man, just once, I'd like to meet someone who's excited about this from the get-go. Here's the thing, Kat. You can fly. You can literally fly. You were doing it before I caught you and helped you out a bit. Haven't you always dreamed of flying?"

I only asked, "Am I stuck looking like this forever?"

He said, "Did I look like this when we met?"

I said, "No, you were hot as hell." I winced. I was being honest, but I really wasn't in the mood to hit on him right now.

He grinned. Then he winked and said, "Thank you. I'm hot this way, too. Just literally."

I screamed and twisted out of the way of the fire that spouted out of his mouth in a quick poof. He said, "Stop squirming. You think you became the one dragon that's not impervious to fire?"

Then he blew a big blast right over my shoulders. It felt… amazing. Like a hot water bath, or one of those hot stone treatments at a massage parlor.

I purred. Involuntarily, of course. A satisfied, soft grumble came out of my long throat and in return, CC purred, too.

He kept pouring fire over my body, and I kept making soft, happy noises.

We alighted on top of a tree. We were in the branches again. He let me find my own footing before he let go of me.

I saw the fullness of him. He was a dragon, from the top of his head to his toes – his talons.

A tail. I looked down at myself. He was right, we did look similar, except he was a ruby red and I was a forest green.

I said, "What the hell am I? If you say I'm a dragon, I'm going to murder you, because I already get that part."

He held his dragon paws up in a 'we cool; gesture and said, "It's important to cover the basics. But more specifically, you're what's called a shifter. You can change, whenever you want, between your boring human form and your way cooler dragon form."

I said, "Okay, fine. Let's say I accept that bit of lunacy and don't assume the rational thing, which is that you slipped hallucinogens in my drinks. I didn't want to change into a dragon. So why did it happen?"

He said, "Okay, this is harder to explain to girls. But look at it like this. You know how when young boys get erections, they can't control them? Or make them go away? The feeling happens and it's happening. As they get older, they can ignore it, or make it happen by thinking about certain things? They get control over it."

I sat for a moment. I said, incredulously, "You're telling me becoming a dragon is like a weird erection for me? I don't know how to control my dragon hard-on yet?"

He nodded happily.

I said, "Does anyone know you're like this?"

He said, "My whole gang is made up of shifters. Well, shifters and, shall we say – to be delicate – dragon enthusiasts."

I could've laughed, if I'd remembered how to do that. Enthusiasts?

I looked down at my hands. I didn't have the urge to laugh anymore.

Then the voice in my head said so softly, it was like a lullaby, only it woke me up instead of drew me to sleep, "Do you want to learn how to fly? Like, really fly?"

No matter how much I hated myself in that moment, how in the hell do you say no to something like that?

Chapter Eight

I woke up to sunshine, cut by the partially open shades on the window. The smooth white blanket on top of me was made for sterility, not comfort. I was in a crinkly hospital gown with the back open.

It didn't take a genius to figure out where I was. Why I was there took a little bit more detective work.

We'd been flying, right? He'd been showing me, on bigger and bigger trees, how to land. Then we found a huge one.

I was petrified. This was one of those old-ass Montana forest trees that have probably been there since fish first grew legs and walked around topside.

CC was staring at me with hungry eyes. Every leap we made, his breathing got heavier. I doubted it was the exertion, since he did all of the leaps so smoothly.

He was impressed with me. Every chance I took was turning him on.

The feeling of flight was like nothing else. It had all the exhilaration of a rollercoaster and the smooth replenishing feeling of swimming in clear, smooth water. It was the biggest rush of power I'd ever had.

I guess the only thing I could really compare it to would be skiing. When you skied, it felt as if you owned the slopes. As if you were part of the wind and also all of the nature that had given itself up to you.

As I swooped and dove, I felt I was a true apex predator. But the landings always brought me back some humility. I was clunky, and each time I felt as if I was falling off a bike, and I could feel the bruises and bumps under my tough, scaly exterior.

But, here I was, about to jump off a tree as tall as a small mountain (at least it felt like it), ride the wave of aerodynamics, and come to some kind of stop at the bottom. CC said it was all about trusting yourself to make the landing, or at least trusting yourself to survive if it went awry.

Surfing always sounded insane to me. Getting out onto the water and praying it didn't smash your face in, all so you can get a few minutes of adrenaline rush. Really only a few seconds.

As I looked into CC's eyes, I thought I understood. I stepped off the tree and flapped my massive wings to get air resistance. They felt great as they unfolded and hit the warm summer air. The air filled my large lungs, and the high I felt was ten times better than the runner's highs I chased in high school on the track team.

CC was a second behind me. We looped in the air, dancing around each other on the rhythm of the wind. Occasionally, one of us would bathe the other in a delicious blast of fire.

Then, he got a devilish look in his eye. "Let's play," he said, "Tag."

He blasted me with a full cannonball of fire, and I roared with the playful joy of it. I chased him, and he flew back into the tree line, testing my agility. I wasn't about to give up. He was clearly slowing himself down so I had a chance, which made it all the more important that I catch him. I sent blasts carefully through the trees, trying to hit him without hitting any extremely flammable wood.

Eventually I had him trapped so he had to rush across a road. I followed closely behind him. That was when I became enveloped in a white light and felt a harsh smash into my ribcage. I heard him scream my name, in my mind. Then all went quiet.

I woke up in the hospital. Blake was sitting across from me, concerned as all hell but relieved to see me awake.

Maybe it was all a dream? Is that what I wanted?

To have never really flown?

Chapter Nine

Blake rushed over to my side and grabbed my hand. I almost recoiled, but then I saw that my hand was completely normal.

Maybe it had all been a dream. What had really happened, then?

I looked up into Blake's soft, brown eyes and waited for some kind of explanation. He looked as if he was going to cry.

He said, "Kat? Are you awake? Can you hear me?"

I said, "Yeah, I'm awake. I feel fine. Why the hell am I in a hospital bed?"

He exhaled, as if he'd been holding his breath all night.

"Oh my God, Kat, I was out looking for you. I was driving down the road, when all of a sudden this huge thing sprinted out of the trees. At least I thought it was huge. I didn't even have time to swerve – it was as if it flew right in front of me. But, when I got out of the car, it looked as if I had hit you. But it didn't look like you. That is, it only partly looked like you."

Oh no. It wasn't a dream. It was all very real.

He continued, "I could tell it was you, but there was something wrong with your body. It was all green and twisted. I thought I'd killed you, Kat. So I drove you straight to the hospital."

He had seen me like that, partially shifted, and had driven me to a hospital. Because he saw what I really was.

I was a monster, and I could shift back at any moment.

He ran his hands through his fluffy blond hair, which looked like a halo in the sunlight. He said, "It must sound as if I'm drunk, because, clearly, you're fine. Maybe I hit something else and then found you. The doctors said you'd been drinking. I don't know how to explain what I saw. I must've been out of my mind, because I thought I'd killed you. Katherine, you're the most important person in my world, and I thought I'd killed you."

I had so many warring emotions. Yesterday, I had wanted nothing more than to hear this. But so much had happened since then.

So much that he'd never understand.

Clearly, he couldn't sense that. He got on to his knees at the side of the bed and looked up at me.

With a tremble in his voice, he said, "Katherine. It's always been you. I've met other girls and I've traveled around, but you know where my mind always goes back to? Walking through the woods with you. Yesterday, when you ran off, I felt so stupid. The whole time I had wanted to tell you how I felt, but my tongue was tied into a knot. How do I take a lifetime and drill it into one sentence, so you understand? So I understand? It took me all these years of your being gone to realize … You're it. I want you to be it for the rest of my life."

He'd gotten carried away. He clearly hadn't wanted to say that much.

He smiled that honey-butter smile.

He said, "After a lifetime already, of being your best friend, I want to see where this can go. If we take the training wheels off. I want to see what happens if we just go where things take us naturally."

Little did he know what happened to my body when nature took over. I was getting nervous. Were my hands changing color?

I hoped I was imagining that. What would happen if I shifted right in front of him? I imagined it would not be a pretty process.

I couldn't let him see it. Where could I go? Where in the world could I hide?

I looked out of the window, toward the sky. The first and only place I really felt powerful.

Out in the parking lot was a slender, handsome man in black leather. He was waiting next to his bike, looking at my window. At least it seemed as if he was.

Because how could he know I was in here?

Right. The telepathy thing. Did that still work when we weren't in dragon form?

"Yeah, it super does," he said, and winked at me, "Waiting for you, boo."

I looked at Blake. He was breathless, searching my face for a response.

Then he jumped back in without letting me respond, "Maybe this is all too sudden. I get it. I think I'm just making sure I say it now, because when I saw you crumpled up on the ground, I thought I'd totally lost my chance to ever say it."

I nodded. I said, "I thought I'd lost my chance with you when I ran into the woods like a madwoman."

He smiled, "Hey, you ran away from a horrible date. I was awful. I barely talked the whole time. You must've thought I hated you or something. Truth is, I just didn't know how to say all of this. But I had plenty of time to think about it while driving around the forest looking for you."

He rubbed my hand gently. His hands were warm, but not as warm as CC's fire on my back.

He said, "Do you think you could … Forgive me?"

I nearly jumped. "Forgive you? What for? Being sweet?"

He shook his head, "For being a dope. And the bad date. Give me a chance at another date? Let's start over?"

I smiled. A lump grew in my throat.

A chance to start over. God, I'd love that.

Except I didn't have that kind of chance. There wasn't any going back from the knowledge I'd gained last night.

Once you learn how to fly, you can't forget it.

I swallowed the lump and told him, "Of course." I needed him to feel comfortable leaving the room, so I could get out of there. Head to CC.

His phone rang, interrupting the absolutely blissful expression on his face. He checked it, with annoyance, until he saw who it was.

"Your parents," he said, showing me the number, as if I wouldn't believe him. He flipped it open and rushed from the room, telling both me and them, "I'll be right down to get you. She's up now, thank God."

He had left the room. I had even less time, now, to make my escape. Once my parents came in, I didn't think I'd be strong enough to leave them.

I couldn't put them through this. Whatever this was.

I thought, "So how do I get out of here?"

CC shrugged. "Jump."

I frowned. "I don't have any clothes."

CC said, "Totally fine with that." I stuck my tongue out at him. He said, "I brought you an outfit, just in case you were squeamish about it." He patted the folded pile on the seat next to him.

I struggled for a second with the window before finding the lock and popping it open.

As I leapt, I tried not to think about how Blake and my parents would feel when they entered an empty hospital room – the window open and letting in the summer heat.

Chapter Ten

We barely got out of the parking lot before CC started doing dumb shit.

He weaved through the traffic like a madman. I clutched at his stomach, from my position behind him on the bike, feeling whatever caused the shift in me bubble up in response to my fear.

I yelled directly into his ear, "Stop driving like you're trying to die!"

He shouted back, "Uh, what are you so worried about? You literally got hit by a car last night."

I guessed he was right. I was fine, despite having been rammed into by a pickup truck.

My voice was already hoarse from trying to shout against the speed of the wind, so instead I thought, "But I was in dragon form when that happened. It protected me."

He responded, "You're always a dragon. It's just that sometimes you don't look like it."

As if to prove his point, in the most ludicrous way possible, he took a sudden left turn, too sudden to handle with the bike, and it rolled.

It threw me off of it. I tried to keep a grip on CC's chest, but the force was too much, and I was torn off. I flew through the air in a totally not fun way, and came to a harsh stop against a tree.

I lay on the forest floor by the highway. No cars were going by, so nobody would stop and help us. I looked at CC, where he was sitting up against a tree, laughing, but clearly in pain.

I screamed, "What the hell? What were you thinking? You could have killed both of us."

He smiled and put a hand on his heart, a mocking version of an apology. "I've done that trick a thousand times," he said, "I did it the day I met you. I knew we'd be fine."

I felt all over my body. He was right. I had some bumps, sure, but nothing worse than tripping over when you're walking.

Except when he took his hand off his chest, I saw it had the sheen of blood on it. Ruby red, like his skin when he was a dragon.

I gasped, and ran toward him.

I said, "Did you hit a tree or something?"

He snorted. "No," he said, "I pissed you off."

"What does that mean?" I asked, terrified.

He said, "Your hand turned into a claw and tried to dig into me when we got thrown. I guess it's only fair, I was messing with you. I didn't think you'd shift that fast, though."

My heart jumped into my throat and got stuck there. He had a nasty slash across his chest.

Had I killed him in my fear? Had I ruined that beautiful body because I didn't want to trust him, or trust that I could take a fall?

Tears threatened to choke my voice, and my skin itched. I couldn't let all that primal energy take over now. That's what had cut him up in the first place.

I choked out, "What do I do?" I looked frantically toward the road.

He smiled. "You've still got a ton to learn about this whole dragon thing. When an animal gets wounded, it doesn't go toward civilization. It goes toward water. There's a spring in the forest a little bit west of here. Let's head there. I can wash out this wound and let it heal up before we rejoin the group."

I helped him stand up and carried most of his weight toward where he pointed. I couldn't believe how easy he was to lift.

He laughed, and then said telepathically, "We've got bird bones. It's how our bulky bodies can get airborne."

I didn't want to think about us as dragons, right now. I wanted to remember everything I'd ever learned from CPR or First Aid training.

We got to the spring fairly quickly, since it wasn't all that difficult to help him along.

It was beautiful. Sunlight dappled the dewy green grass, while flowers swayed in the slight breeze. A small waterfall, only a few feet high, added a charming, relaxing babble to the sweet pastoral scene.

CC hobbled a few steps away from me. He stripped off his tight leather jacket, and tore his bloody, already ripped t-shirt in half. The sunlight danced on his warm skin, and even the ruby red blood looked like a decorative sash across his perfect torso.

Then I heard the zip of his pants. I knew that for propriety's sake I should probably look away. But when he slipped down his pants, it was all I could do not to gawk.

He was massive. The sight of it was almost comical against his slender, athletic hips and lean but delicious ass. I wondered how he managed to fit into those tight leather pants in the first place.

As I stared at him, the heat and pulsing from my pussy became unbearable. I knew if anyone touched me down there, they might get a third degree burn.

God, I wanted him to touch me.

He turned around, tossing that movie star smile at me as if it wasn't a precious gift to be savored and adored.

"Hop on in," he said, and skipped into the spring.

I slipped out of my own messy, torn clothes and followed willingly.

Chapter Eleven

He was relaxing in the water while I felt anything but relaxed. It was all I could do not to jump on him and ride him. But his chest needed to heal, and I wanted to respect that.

Until he said, "Hey, you've got something in your eye."

I said, "What?"

Then he splashed. A major swipe of water fell over me and into my face.

I wrinkled my nose and wiped my face. "Of course you know, this means war," I said in my best imitation of Bugs Bunny.

The splash battle was breathless and violent. I'd like to say I came out the victor, but he had a massive slash wound on his chest, so I couldn't take too much pride in it. In order to assert my dominance in splashing, I held him under the water, dunking him like a middle school bully.

Until he pushed his face in between my legs, under the water. He propelled me toward the side of the pool, and before I could say, "I win," he was licking my pulsing clit with an unbearable fervor.

I was trying to keep quiet, since we'd already been yelling as we played in the water and I didn't want to attract any hunters or animals, but then he bit my thigh with vicious joy and I yelped.

After that, all bets were off. I screamed as he gripped my ass and my thighs and licked me up and down. He came up for air, only rarely, and I marveled at his lung capacity.

That was, I guess, until he couldn't stand it anymore and he appeared above the water. But he was still licking. Licking up my naked body while pressing his hard cock against my thighs.

When he got to my breasts I wasn't even breathing anymore. I concentrated 100% on how wonderful my body felt. He licked the curves of my breasts, which looked massive and enlarged from his passionate attention.

He spent a long time, a tormenting amount of time, licking all around my breasts and squeezing them. He pressed his knee up against my pussy so I could grind against him while he played with my breasts. I thought that would relieve some of the pressure I felt but it only intensified how badly I wanted him inside me.

Then his tongue flickered across my nipples. My whole body reacted as if I'd been shocked. He licked and squeezed my nipples and I started begging.

I said, "Please, please, please, get inside me, I want you, please." I was using human language but I didn't feel human anymore. I felt like an animal that needed this pleasure.

He needed it too. I could tell, because when I grabbed his cock and tried to pull him toward me, it was engorged and pulsing violently.

As soon as I touched his penis, making sure to run my palm over its head and squeeze it, he didn't play any more games.

He pushed himself inside me with a force I'd never known. I kept my hips pushed against him with a steady pressure, so that every pounding thrust had maximum depth. I wanted all of him, and I told him so, although I wasn't sure if I was speaking telepathically or out loud.

I felt absolutely filled up by his magnificent cock, and the power of his thrusts drove me crazy. Especially since he kept biting my neck and licking my tits as he pushed into me, which only served to heighten the pleasure into a painful starburst.

As if to highlight how we had become nothing more than animals rutting in the water, he pulled out of me and flipped me over. He shoved his hard cock rapidly, punching my G spot and making me scream out his name as I braced myself against the side of the spring.

It was mind blowing, and as he continued to fill me up with unimaginable pleasure. He smacked my ass with a harsh open palm. It all felt so good, and I screamed for him to do it even harder. He did, and the wild passion turned my screams into bloody roars.

I was coming, forced to the edge of passion by the onslaught of his amazing cock. My pussy clenched tighter than anyone had ever made it tighten before.

He said, "Oh God, Kat, you're so tight. You're going to make me come."

Suddenly I wanted more than anything to be filled with his semen. The idea of his burning hot whiteness filling my belly was startlingly sexy. Hearing him groan and imagining him finish inside me brought me to climax.

I screamed, pressing myself against his hot form in the water as all of me convulsed. Waves of pleasure sprang out from my vagina into my whole body, until it felt as if even my fingernails were coming. It all turned into a wonderful, peaceful feeling of being completely wrung out and smacked raw.

I was totally satisfied, but he was still groaning. He pulled out of me with a whimper, and in my breathlessness the sight of it made me want him again.

I said, "You know, I am on the pill."

He shook his head. "As much as I want that, you have no idea how powerful dragon sperm is. It doesn't really care about human medicine."

His chest had healed. I felt so grateful for that, I got on my knees in the water, and I licked his shimmering member.

I started by licking the head of it, but once I heard his groans, I got too excited to hold back or strategize. So I thrust his massive cock as far as I could down my throat, smashing it into the back of my mouth, while he made marvelous, joyful noises that sounded absolutely shocked at how good it felt.

When he screamed out, "I'm coming, Kat, I'm coming right in your mouth," I used the last reserves of my energy to push his cock as deep as I could down my throat.

When his semen came out, it was an immense amount. Imagine chugging boiling water. I just opened my throat and let it come, and I started rubbing my clit as I enjoyed the feeling of his orgasm.

I came again just as he finished ejaculating, and we pulled back from each other. I licked my lips, not unlike how he licked it that night of the party (wow, only just the day before. How quickly things change), and he stared down at me with surprise.

He said, "You win," and fell back into the water, where he pretended to fall unconscious.

I laughed, and decided to lie back and enjoy the peacefulness of the forest in my own post-orgasmic, joyful haze.

Chapter Twelve

So, I became the main girl of a dragon-shifting, biker-gang leader. Which I think was not what my parents had intended when I had started my aerophysics degree.

Nobody made me feel like CC did. When his eyes were on me, I was filled with a violent fire, unlike anything I'd ever felt before, and I needed him right then, wherever we were. We often got left behind by the gang, because we'd pulled off to canoodle in a roadside clearing or up in a massive tree.

I was sitting on his lap in a biker bar. We were on the outskirts of Montana, maybe a little closer to Idaho than I'd been before. My leather miniskirt was riding up a lot more than I wanted, but it felt weird to be wearing anything other than what passed as our uniform, I guess.

I was nursing a beer, which was flat and not particularly good, while CC chatted with a guy and girl I didn't recognize. Some locals who were falling for his usual schtick. I didn't pay much attention, because I'd heard the stories before.

My mind was somewhere else. I hated myself for it, because here I was on the adventure of the lifetime, literally having sex while flying on a nightly basis with a gorgeous boy, and my dumb brain couldn't help drifting to the golden-haired dream I'd left at home.

The first time Blake and I had kissed was in middle school. It was a mess, because I had a retainer that made me store up too much saliva in my mouth, and he had floppy emo hair (still blond though, he never dyed it because his mom would've been too sad) that hung in his eyes and disrupted his vision.

We were 'dating' in that timid way that twelve year olds date. We were hanging outside a Target, waiting for my mom to come pick us up. All the other kids who we'd been loitering with had already gone home.

So we were alone. Which we had been a lot of times. But this time it felt different, because this was the first time we'd been alone since we had called ourselves boyfriend and girlfriend.

I didn't know what to do. Then he asked me, "Do you think I'm a good boyfriend? Like, do you feel happy when we're together?"

I nodded my head. "Of course!" I said, swallowing some spit. I felt a lot of things when we were together. Mostly tense during that brief dating period, but at the time I thought that was what being in love felt like.

I nodded resolutely. "You're a great boyfriend," I said, then quickly panicked, and asked, "Am I a good girlfriend?"

"Yep. You're awesome," he said, with a firm nod, "You're really funny."

I relaxed. He looked at me. I looked at him.

We had a horrible kiss where I literally drooled out of the side of my mouth. It wasn't very magical.

What was magical was the ride back to his place, where he let his hand rest on mine, but barely, so that my mom wouldn't see.

I think we broke up a few weeks later because we didn't want to 'ruin our friendship', which was also exciting because it felt very mature and grown up to break up for such a smart reason, and so amicably.

Sitting on CC's lap in the bar, I felt like crying. I got up, and he smacked my ass, so I turned around and nearly pushed him off the chair.

He held his hands up. "Sorry! Sorry, baby. What's up?"

I said, "I need some air." He tried to hand me cigarettes, as if they would calm me down, but I pushed them away and ran outside.

A golden head of hair was waiting for me there.

Blake was outside the bar, leaning against his pick-up truck.

He said, "I thought these were your bikes, but I couldn't be sure. I couldn't work up the courage to go in."

I didn't know what to say. I suddenly hated my outfit. It was so very not-me.

Blake didn't waste a second looking me over. He walked straight up to me and hugged me, and as I melted into his arms, I started to cry.

He whispered to me, "Your dad told me that … You're a shifter. That you have this gift. He has it, too. He says he should've told you, told all of us, and you never would have run away."

Blake's large body started shaking, and I realized he was crying with me as he held me tightly.

"My … my dad?" I whispered.

He said, "Yes. It's genetic. He told me all about it, and you know what? It's pretty freaking weird, Kat. But somehow … it makes sense for you? You've always been special. Not just to me, but to everybody. This is just another way you're special. God damn it, I love you, Katherine. I've been trying to find you for months, now, so I could tell you. Whatever you are, whoever you want to be, I love you."

I tipped my head back to look up at his face and saw how sincere he was. He bent down and kissed me softly, the lightest brush against my lips. Then he pulled back.

He said, "I know you might feel better with people more like you. Like this motorcycle club. But I wanted you to know … You have a choice. You can come home and be you, and be loved, or you can stay here, and be you, and be with them. Whichever you want, it's your choice."

It was too much. It was all too crazy. I'd already chosen this life, and I didn't want to think about it anymore.

I stepped away from him. Away from home.

I told him, "Thank you. So much. But I can't."

I went back inside and left him by his pickup truck.

I tried to find CC, so he could look me in the eye and remind me why I'd chosen this life of freedom over Blake and small town Montana.

I asked someone where he was, and they just laughed. I got an awful, sticky feeling in my throat.

I rushed to the bathroom. I threw open the door to the men's room, which CC hadn't even bothered to lock. He was getting blown by the dude he'd been talking to earlier, while the girl made out with him and squealed while he fingered her.

I shouted, "CC, what the hell?"

He stopped kissing the girl long enough to say, "Care to join?"

Then I realized what a biker gang meant by "main girl". It meant I was his primary, but not his only. And I knew him well enough to know that he would never, ever change.

I'd made a huge mistake. The one true love of my life had just driven off in a pickup.

But it wasn't that hard to catch up when you could fly.

I rushed out of the door, starting to feel the burn on my shoulders as I geared up to shift, only to find that Blake was still sitting in his car. He hadn't pulled away yet.

He hadn't even put the key in the ignition. He looked at me, waiting breathlessly.

I walked to the passenger door and slid inside. He stared at me, cautiously, not wanting to expect too much.

I said, "On a scale of one to one hundred, how pissed is my mom?"

He grimaced and shook his head. "One billion."

I said, "Awesome."

We held hands the whole drive home.

Epilogue

Blake and I got married in his parents' backyard, which had beautiful apple trees and an adorable pond. In all the pictures, we look perfect and happy.

Most days, I feel perfect and happy. I finished my degree and now I work with Blake's dad in his mountain laboratory, ironically studying mountain air currents and their effect on flight.

I almost never shift. It just doesn't fit in the perfect lifestyle that Blake and I are building. We've bought our own little house with a pond in the backyard. We're thinking about having kids, although I'm not sure we shouldn't just adopt, if the whole shifter thing is genetic.

But sometimes, when I dream … I see the night sky from the view of a dragon. And Blake doesn't talk about it, but I whisper somebody else's name … Because he's the only face I see in my dreams.

CC. The one who taught me how to fly.

www.ingramcontent.com/pod-product-compliance
Lightning Source LLC
Chambersburg PA
CBHW020506160726
47991CB00007B/2824